Bramble Bear

I wish I was...

by Geoffrey Alan

illustrated by Pamela Storey

BRIMAX · NEWMARKET · ENGLAND

"I do not want to be a bear today," sighs Bramble.
"I wish I was a bird. Then I could fly!"
He flaps his chubby little arms and runs down the hill, pretending to take off.
But he slips and roly-polies all the way to the bottom.
"Ohh!" he gasps, landing in thick grass.

"Now my head is buzzing!" he mutters. But then he sees a bee collecting pollen from a flower beside him.
"So you are making that buzzing noise!" grins Bramble. "Your black and yellow stripes are very smart. If I were a bee, I would make as much honey as possible!"

As the bee flies off, Bramble chases it until it enters a hollow tree-stump.

"Is that where you hide your honey?" asks Bramble.

"I'm sure you will not miss just a little bit."

Bramble pushes his paw into the tree. But he pulls it out very quickly. There are lots of bees in there. Now they are cross. They chase Bramble.

Bramble rushes towards a waterfall. He hurries underneath it. SPLASH! Water pours all over him but he stays there until, at last, all the bees fly away.
Poor Bramble steps out. He sits in the sun to dry his fur. "I'm glad I'm not a bee," he nods. "They get very cross indeed!"

Just then, something hops on to Bramble's tummy.

"A frog!" he smiles. "That's what I want to be. Hopping looks fun!"

The frog hops down and Bramble begins hopping, too. But he lands in some sticky mud. SPLOP!

"Oo . . . er!" he frowns. "Being a frog is very messy!"

Next moment, Bramble feels
something hit his head.
"Sorry!" calls a squirrel.
"I dropped the nut I was eating.
I will go and get another one."
Bramble gasps, amazed, as
he sees the squirrel leap from
branch to branch.
"If I were a squirrel, I could do
that!" he dreams.

"Wait for me!" calls Bramble, beginning to climb the tree. He follows the squirrel along a branch. But Bramble is too heavy and the branch starts to bend.

Bramble looks down and feels dizzy. The ground seems a long way down. Suddenly, the branch breaks and Bramble falls into some big, leafy ferns.

"Trees are very high things," Bramble says, looking up at the tree. "I'm glad I'm not a squirrel. I prefer being on the ground."
"Sssso do I," hisses a snake, slithering past.
Bramble lies on his tummy and tries to wriggle, too. But he cannot move from the same spot. "I couldn't be a snake," he puffs. "I would never get anywhere!"

"Let me help you," says a deer, towering over Bramble. "Hold on to my antlers." The deer pulls Bramble to his feet.

"Thank you," replies Bramble. "Your antlers are useful. I wish I had some."

Bramble finds two branches and holds them to his head. 'Now I have antlers, too!' he thinks. Bramble trots along. But his antlers catch on a bush.

Bramble pulls and pushes, heaves and huffs to free the branch. Next moment, he falls into the bush. Poor Bramble completely disappears. Slowly, he clambers out again. "I don't think I want antlers, after all," says Bramble. "They get hooked on to things!"

Bramble pulls and pushes, heaves and huffs to free the branch. Next moment, he falls into the bush. Poor Bramble completely disappears. Slowly, he clambers out again. "I don't think I want antlers, after all," says Bramble. "They get hooked on to things!"

"Bramble! BRAMBLE!"
he hears his Mother call.
"Coming!" he says, brushing
bits of leaf from his fur.
Bramble's Mother is waiting
on the doorstep, wiping her
paws on her apron. When she
sees Bramble, she shakes
her head.
"What a mess you look!
What have you been doing?"
she asks.

Indoors, Bramble explains while his Mother dries him after a bath.

"I was playing being other animals," he sighs. He tells his Mother everything that has happened to him.

She smiles and brushes his fur. "Your thick fur helped to save you from being stung by the bees," she says, "and from hurting yourself when you fell."

"It also stopped you getting scratched and catching a cold as it dries quickly," she adds. In no time, Bramble is the cleanest bear again. He sniffs freshly baked honey-cake. "Mm! I'm pleased I'm me, after all," he tells his Mother. "I have decided, I like being a bear!"

Say these words again

wriggle	fly
antler	stripes
hooked	honey
doorstep	shivers
thick	sticky
sniffs	dreams
hollow	branch